Princess PULVERIZER

Quit BUGGIN' me!

PENGUIN WORKSHOP
Penguin Young Readers Group
An Imprint of Penguin Random House LLC

Text copyright © 2018 by Nancy Krulik. Illustrations copyright © 2018 by Ben Balistreri. All rights reserved. Published by Penguin Workshop, an imprint of Penguin Random House LLC, 345 Hudson Street, New York, New York 10014. PENGUIN and PENGUIN WORKSHOP are trademarks of Penguin Books Ltd, and the W colophon is a trademark of Penguin Random House LLC. Printed in the USA.

Library of Congress Cataloging-in-Publication Data is available.

ISBN 9780515158403 (pbk)   10 9 8 7 6 5 4 3 2 1
ISBN 9780515158410 (hc)   10 9 8 7 6 5 4 3 2 1

NANCY KRULIK

PRINCESS PULVERIZER

Quit BUGGIN' me!

art by Ben Balistreri

Penguin Workshop
An Imprint of Penguin Random House

For Josie, who really loves grilled cheese—or any other "people food"—NK

To my fourth golden retriever, Fatty Lumpkin. When life gets difficult, you can always be counted on to remind me what's truly important. Food—BB

CHAPTER 1

"I wanna play! I wanna play!" Dribble shouted excitedly.

The ground shook beneath the big green dragon as he jumped up and down. He pointed toward the group of kids who had gathered in the middle of the town square. "I bet I can break that piñata with one swing!" he boasted.

"I don't think those kids need any help," Dribble's best friend, a knight-in-training named Lucas, said. "That last kid got really close to hitting it."

But Dribble didn't hear Lucas. He was already halfway down the road, bouncing toward the square, shouting, *"I wanna play! I wanna play!"*

"I wish he would stop jumping." Princess Pulverizer groaned, tossing her long braid over her shoulder. "All this shaking is giving me a bellyache."

"That could also be from the four grilled cheddar cheese on rye sandwiches you had for breakfast," Lucas pointed out.

Princess Pulverizer shrugged. "Dribble makes delicious grilled cheese. I couldn't help myself." The earth shook beneath her feet. "Whoa!" she exclaimed.

"That *was* a big one," Lucas agreed.

"Come on," Princess Pulverizer urged him. "We better catch up to Dribble before he breaks something. And I don't mean the piñata."

"AAAAAHHHHHHH!"

Princess Pulverizer and Lucas reached the town square in time to see all the children running off to hide—leaving Dribble alone by the piñata.

"I just wanted to play with them," Dribble said sadly, looking around the empty square.

"It's probably time for their lunch," Lucas said, trying to spare his feelings.

Dribble shook his head. "That's not it. They're scared of me because I'm a

dragon. Which is ridiculous. I
wouldn't hurt anyone. Do I look
scary to you?"

Dribble smiled broadly and bared his
big teeth. Then he fluttered his eyelashes
over his big, bulging eyes.

Princess Pulverizer gulped. Dribble
didn't just look scary. He looked a little
crazy, too.

"I wonder where we are," she said,
trying to change the subject. "I've never
been to this kingdom before."

The princess began to walk around the square, searching for a sign that might give her a clue as to her whereabouts. As she passed by a big bale of hay, she heard whispering.

"Do you think that big green thing is the Yabko-kokomo Beast?" one voice said.

"I don't know," someone else whispered back. "But we better stay here till he leaves, just in case. We don't want to be the next kids from Yabko-kokomo to be captured and dragged off into the forest."

Princess Pulverizer hurried back to where Lucas and Dribble were standing. "We're in a place called Yabko-kokomo," she told them.

"How did you find that out?" Lucas asked her. He looked around. "I don't see any signs or anything."

"I have my ways," Princess Pulverizer replied mysteriously. "I also learned why the kids all ran away, Dribble. And it's not because you're a dragon."

"It's not?" Dribble sounded surprised. "Well, that's good."

"They ran away because they think you're the Yabko-kokomo Beast," said Princess Pulverizer. "They think you capture people and drag them away."

"What?" Dribble's voice scaled up

angrily. A burst of fire escaped through his mouth. "Why would they think that?"

"I have no idea," Princess Pulverizer said with a grin.

"That's horrible," Dribble said. "Why are you smiling?"

"I'm smiling because there are people who have been kidnapped and need help," Princess Pulverizer said. "And we're just the ones to help them."

"Wh-why us?" Lucas asked nervously. "I don't want to fight a beast. Beasts are scary."

"How do you know?" Princess Pulverizer asked. "Have you ever met one?"

"I'm not sure," Lucas admitted. "What does a beast look like?"

Dribble shook his head at Princess

Pulverizer. "You just want to help those people so you can check off another good deed on your Quest of Kindness," he said.

Princess Pulverizer shrugged. "So what? If we rescue the people who have been kidnapped, it's good for them *and* for me. It's really lucky we came by when we did."

Neither Lucas nor Dribble seemed particularly surprised to hear the princess declare she wanted to track down the Yabko-kokomo Beast. That's because Princess Pulverizer wasn't exactly a sweet, gentle, run-of-the-mill princess. She was different.

While other princesses were busy dancing the saltarello at royal balls, Princess Pulverizer was busy battling angry ogres.

While other princesses spent their

days sipping tea with their pinkies in the air, Princess Pulverizer spent *her* days outwitting wicked wizards.

And while other princesses were welcoming princes into their palaces, Princess Pulverizer was vanquishing vicious villains and terrifying tremendous trolls.

Princess Pulverizer didn't even want to *be* a princess. She wanted to be a *knight*. A full-fledged, horseback-riding, armor-wearing, damsel-in-distress-saving kind of knight. But to do that, she would have to go to Knight School.

Her father, King Alexander, had actually said she could go to Knight School—on one condition. She had to complete eight good deeds on a Quest of Kindness and collect tokens of gratitude for each one as proof.

Once she had done that, she could get her first set of armor!

King Alexander had explained that knights were selfless people who spent their lives helping others. A Quest of Kindness would teach Princess Pulverizer to care about other people, the way all good knights should.

So now Princess Pulverizer was traveling the countryside trying to find folks who needed her help.

But doing good deeds was hard work. Luckily, during her travels, Princess Pulverizer had stumbled upon Dribble and Lucas. They were a great help to her, which might surprise a lot of people. After all, Lucas was such a fraidy-cat, the other boys had nicknamed him Lucas the Lily-Livered and laughed him out of

Knight School. But he was loyal and good-hearted, as knights needed to be.

Dribble had been banished from his lair because, unlike other dragons, he used his fire for making grilled cheese sandwiches rather than burning down villages. But if there was anything a princess on a quest needed, it was a good chef—especially one who was also pretty fierce when it came to fighting bad guys.

The princess and her pals had already used their combined talents to defeat three tough enemies. But that still left five good deeds for the princess to accomplish.

Unfortunately, not everyone was anxious to go off in search of an evil beast.

"I don't think it would be a win for *me*," Lucas said. "I don't want to be captured by a beast. And let's face it, if a beast is going to capture one of us, it's bound to be me."

Princess Pulverizer looked at Lucas's rusty suit of armor. She stared at his boots—which appeared to be on the wrong feet. And she watched as he nervously bit at his upper lip. It was true. If anyone were going to be captured, it *would* probably be Lucas.

"We're just going to have to be sure the beast doesn't capture *any* of us," Princess Pulverizer said. "We have to stick together. One little beast can't be a match for the power of three!" She looked down at Lucas's feet. "It might help if you put your shoes on the right feet," she added.

"You probably won't trip as often."

"Why do I get the feeling we're going after this beast no matter what I say?" Lucas asked as he sat down on the ground and removed his boots.

Princess Pulverizer didn't answer. Instead, she started heading down the road.

"Come on, Lucas," Dribble called to his friend. "The sooner we go, the sooner we rescue the captured Yabko-kokomoians . . . or is it Yabko-kokomites?"

"I have no idea," Princess Pulverizer admitted. "I just know we have to find them. Come on, Lucas. Let's go."

"Okay." Lucas surrendered. He turned around quickly and . . .

CLANK! His visor fell down over his eyes.

"Hey! Who turned out the lights?"

Lucas shouted. He stumbled in the
darkness, struggling with the visor. "I
think it's stuck." He groaned. "I can't—"

SMASH! Lucas rammed right into the
piñata. The clay cracked, and the candy
and toys began spilling all over the place.

Kids came running from every corner of
the square.

"Whoa!" Lucas shouted as he lost
his balance and fell down onto the
cobblestones below.

The force of the fall knocked Lucas's
visor loose. "Ouch," he moaned
as he lifted it, stood,

and walked over to his friends.

"Those kids don't seem so frightened anymore," Dribble huffed. "Some people will do anything for a sweet treat."

"Maybe they realized you're not so scary after all," Lucas said, trying to be kind.

Dribble walked a little closer to the fallen treats and toys. He picked up a whirligig and blew hard at its pretty colored blades.

Whoosh! A small flame shot out of his mouth. The toy went up in smoke.

"Yikes!" one of the kids shouted as he ran off.

Dribble looked at the charred whirligig stick in his claw.

"I gotta watch the pepper jack cheese," he said. "It gives me heartburn."

"Come on, you guys," Princess Pulverizer urged. "Let's get out of here. We have Yabko-kokomians to save."

"Are you sure it's not Yabko-kokom*ites*?" Dribble began. "Or even Yabko-kokomo*ers*?"

Princess Pulverizer shook her head. "Don't start that again. No matter what they're called, we have to save them."

Dribble nodded in agreement and walked alongside the princess in silence. Lucas hurried to keep up, his rusty armor clanging with each step.

Princess Pulverizer frowned as she led her friends down the path. She knew she was being bossy. She also knew knights weren't *supposed* to be bossy.

There had to be a better way to get people to do what she wanted.

But there would be time enough to figure out how to do that—after they'd defeated the Yabko-kokomo Beast!

CHAPTER 2

"Whoops!" Lucas shouted out. His metal suit clanged loudly as he hit the ground, rear end first.

"Shhhh . . . ," Princess Pulverizer warned him. "We don't want to alert the beast if he's hiding in this apple orchard."

"Sorry," Lucas apologized. "I tripped going around that big hole."

"There are *a lot* of holes in this orchard," Dribble said. "And some of them are huge." He pointed to a giant hole near his foot. "You could fit a whole kid in there. Well, a human kid, anyway. We dragons are way too big."

"D-d-do you think the Yabko-kokomo Beast dug these holes?" Lucas asked nervously.

"Nah." Princess Pulverizer shook her head. "I think they were made by animals. Maybe moles."

"Those would have to be really big moles," Lucas said.

"Maybe they're small moles with really big shovels," Princess Pulverizer suggested with a laugh.

GRUMBLE! RUMBLE!

Suddenly, a loud, angry sound filled the air.

Lucas jumped. "Oh no! It's the Yabko-kokomo Beast!" he exclaimed.

Dribble's green cheeks began to flush pink. "No it's not," he admitted. "That was my stomach. I'm hungry. It's been a long time since breakfast."

"I could go for a nice grilled brie on sourdough bread," Princess Pulverizer suggested.

"You know what's better than a grilled cheese sandwich?" Dribble asked.

"Um . . . nothing?" Lucas tried.

"Nope," Dribble said. "A grilled cheese and *apple* sandwich. Luckily there are plenty of apples around here."

"But all these signs say Private Property and Keep Out," Lucas said nervously. "Maybe we should forget the apples."

"There are so many apples on these trees," Dribble countered. "The person

who owns this orchard won't miss one or two."

"But what if the orchard is owned by the Yabko-kokomo Beast?" Lucas asked nervously. "Stealing his apples will make him angry."

Princess Pulverizer reached up, grabbed an apple off one of the trees, and took a bite. "I haven't seen one hint of a beast anywhere," she told Lucas.

"Can you finish chewing before you talk?" Dribble asked her. "You're spraying apple chunks everywhere."

Princess Pulverizer frowned. Dribble sounded just like Lady Frump, her teacher at the Royal School of Ladylike Manners. Still, she swallowed before she spoke again.

"I'm beginning to think maybe there isn't any Yabko-kokomo Beast at all," the princess continued.

"That would be great," Lucas said.

"No it wouldn't," Princess Pulverizer argued. "It would mean a whole day wasted on my Quest of Kindness."

"Not exactly," Dribble said. "People were still captured. And they're still missing."

Princess Pulverizer smiled

broadly. "That's right!" she said excitedly. Then she glanced at Dribble and Lucas. They were giving her some pretty disappointed looks. "I mean, those poor, poor folks," she said, trying desperately to wipe the smile from her face. "We need to look for them."

"Right after lunch, I promise," Lucas told her.

"We'll do a better job of looking for them on full stomachs." Dribble sat down on a huge log and looked around. "I wonder if there are any Granny Smith apples here. Why don't you go find some?" he suggested to the princess.

"Why me?" Princess Pulverizer asked.

"Stop being such a *crab apple*," Dribble said. "Do you want to eat or not?"

Dribble's stomach wasn't the only one

grumbling and rumbling right about now. Princess Pulverizer's was making some *interesting* noises, too.

"I'll pick some low-hanging apples from these trees here," Lucas volunteered. "We all have to pitch in."

"Fine," the princess agreed. "I'll go to that grove over there. And while I'm at it, I'll try and figure out what kind of beast we're dealing with here—because the minute we finish eating, we're getting back on track with this good deed!"

Princess Pulverizer looked behind a cluster of trees. There was no sign of a beast.

She looked down at the muddy ground beneath her. Not a single footprint, other than her own.

She looked up at the sky. There was nothing but a blue jay flying from tree limb to tree limb. (Well, the princess hadn't really expected to find a beast up there, anyway. But you never knew.)

There didn't seem to be any sign of a cruel creature that could be kidnapping the citizens of Yabko-kokomo.

What if there was no

Yabko-kokomo Beast? What if the people who had disappeared had just run away on their own? What if no one needed her help after all?

Then Princess Pulverizer had been wasting her time, that's what.

And if there was one thing she did not have time to waste, it was time. Because she was sick and tired of being called *Princess* Pulverizer. She wanted to be called *Sir* Pulverizer.

Okay, maybe not *sir*. She would have to come up with a different title for herself. But there wasn't time to think about that right now. She grabbed a few apples from a tree, stuffed them in her bag, and started to head back toward where she had left her friends.

"Dribble! Lucas!" Princess Pulverizer shouted as she walked back toward the orchard where she had left her friends. "I found some sour apples. They're not Granny Smiths but . . ."

When Princess Pulverizer reached the log where Dribble had been sitting just a few moments ago, she stopped dead in her tracks. A shiver went down her spine.

Her friends were nowhere to be found. They had simply disappeared—*without a trace.*

CHAPTER 3

Princess Pulverizer searched through the groves of trees.

She peered into bushes.

She looked behind boulders.

But there was no sign of Dribble or
Lucas. And just for a moment, Princess
Pulverizer thought maybe the whole tale
of the Yabko-kokomo Beast was a true
story—that her friends really *had* been
kidnapped.

But then she thought better of it. She
hadn't seen a single sign of a beast. No
matted fur that had been shed on the
ground or caught on the limbs of trees.
No beastly cloven hoofprints in the mud.
Nothing.

So if Lucas and Dribble weren't

kidnapped, what had happened to them? They wouldn't have just left her.

Or would they?

Maybe she'd really crossed the line this time, ordering them around and making them go look for the Yabko-kokomo Beast. She could have been nicer about it. Maybe she drove them away.

No! Dribble and Lucas were loyal. They might be upset with her, but they would never abandon her.

Princess Pulverizer looked down at a deep hole in the earth. Could her friends have been dragged underground?

Well, Lucas might have been. He was scrawny enough to fit into the burrow. But not Dribble. A dragon could never squeeze into there.

So what had happened? Dribble

and Lucas couldn't have disappeared into thin air. Although she didn't see their footprints in the mud, either.

But those could have easily been washed away, because it had started to rain. And not just a little drizzle. This was a full-on, torrential rainstorm. And from the looks of the dark clouds above, there was a lot more coming.

Princess Pulverizer was stuck in a foreign land, in the pouring rain, without a single friend.

For the first time in a really long time, Princess Pulverizer wasn't feeling

brave at all. She was scared. And lonely. All she wanted to do was go home and sleep in her own bed, in her own castle.

The princess wondered if any of her father's Royal Knights of the Skround Table ever felt this way.

There was only one way to find out. She would have to go back to Empiria and ask them.

Sure! That was the answer. She'd go home to Empiria and talk to a few brave knights. Maybe grab a hot meal that *wasn't* a grilled cheese sandwich. And then she could head back out on her Quest of Kindness feeling refreshed and rested. And her next act of kindness would be to find Dribble and Lucas. She would even bring a whole search party with her to help.

It wasn't a bad plan at all.

Except for one thing.

Princess Pulverizer had absolutely no idea how to get back to Empiria from here.

She wasn't even sure where *here* was!

Zing! Just then, a small gnat bit at the princess's face. Ouch. That hurt—like an arrow piercing her cheek.

An arrow! That's it!

Quickly, Princess Pulverizer pulled a long arrow with orange and yellow feathers from her bag. It had been a gift from the mayor of Ire-Mire-Briar-Shire. And if she remembered correctly, the mayor had distinctly told her, "If ever the holder of the arrow finds themselves lost, the arrow will always point them toward home."

Well, Princess Pulverizer was definitely

lost now.
She held the
arrow in the air
and watched as it
wiggled a little to
the left and to the right.
It twitched in front of her.
It pointed over her shoulder. And then
it stopped.

Princess Pulverizer's heart pounded
excitedly. She'd found the way home. All
she had to do was turn around and follow
the arrow.

It seemed to Princess Pulverizer that
she'd been traveling an awfully long time.
It was night now, and she had to squint
to see the magic arrow in the moonlight.

And to make matters worse, she had to watch out for all the giant holes in the ground.

At least the rain had stopped. But she was still sopping wet. Princess Pulverizer couldn't wait to get back to the palace and change into a dry tunic.

The princess followed the arrow to an old wooden fence. The arrow twisted slightly and pointed toward a splintery gate that was falling off its hinges.

Huh? That made no sense. How was going through that gate going to bring her home? But the princess had trusted the arrow this far. So she followed its pointed tip down through the gate.

After a few steps, the arrow drooped and pointed to the ground. The arrow had led the princess to a small, raggedy cottage. The shingles were falling from the roof, and the walls were beginning to crumble. There were bars on all the windows. This was *no* palace.

Stupid arrow! It hadn't led her home at all.

So where *had* it taken her?

CHAPTER 4

Princess Pulverizer walked silently toward the cottage door. She'd put on the ruby ring the Queen of Shmergermeister had given her. The ring had the power to allow whoever was wearing it to walk in silence. No one in the cottage could hear her.

But the princess could sure hear *them*. They were arguing. Loudly.

"You're eating that apple pie awfully quickly!" Princess Pulverizer heard a woman scold. "It took me hours to bake."

"I'm just trying to finish it before I lose my appetite," a man replied angrily. "This pie is so dry, it's turning to dust. You are a terrible chef, Madame Zucker."

"How could anyone cook in such a tiny kitchen with rusty old pans?" Madame Zucker replied. "If you hate my cooking so much, why not let me go?"

"I captured you and brought you here to cook for me," the man said. "And cook for me you shall."

"You eat too much

sugar, Sir Surly," Princess Pulverizer heard a second man's voice scold. "You are going to get a toothache. I've already had to pull half your teeth."

Hmmm . . . *Sir* Surly. There was a knight inside this cottage. Perhaps he could help Princess Pulverizer find her friends. The princess was about to knock on the door when she heard more arguing.

"Dr. Cuspid, could you breathe in the other direction?" Sir Surly demanded. "You're stinking up the whole cottage. It's that onion you ate with your dinner."

"I like onions," Dr. Cuspid insisted. "And my breath wouldn't be so bad if you'd let me grab my toothbrush when you captured me."

"From now on you are only

to eat apples," Sir Surly ordered him. "Try this one."

"I'm tired of apples," Dr. Cuspid complained.

"An apple a day keeps the doctor away," Sir Surly reminded him. "But an onion a day keeps *everyone* away!"

"The last time I heard that joke, I fell off my dinosaur," Madame Zucker replied snidely.

"Speak to me with respect," Sir Surly warned her. "Or else we'll soon be eating Madame Zucker stew—with *Madame Zucker* as the main ingredient."

Princess Pulverizer gasped. Yikes. This guy was really sensitive. She'd never met a knight like that in her father's court.

"AAAAAHHHHH!"

Princess Pulverizer was startled by the

sudden loud shout from inside.

"NATE JAPE, GET THAT SPIDER
AWAY FROM ME!" Sir Surly screamed.
"You know I hate spiders."

"What do you get when you mix a
tarantula with a rose?" the princess
heard a young boy ask.

"What?" Madame Zucker
wondered aloud.

"I don't know," he
said. "But I wouldn't
try smelling it!"
Nate laughed at
his own joke.

But Sir Surly
sure wasn't
laughing.
"I don't

like spider *jokes*, either!" he grumbled.

"Uh-oh," Dr. Cuspid interrupted.

"What now?" Sir Surly demanded.

"I found a worm in this apple," Dr. Cuspid complained.

"Better than finding *half* a worm," Nate Jape joked.

"I don't want to hear another word about worms or spiders," Sir Surly ordered. "I can't stand those creepy creatures."

"What kind of a knight is afraid of bugs?" a new voice piped up.

Whoa, Princess Pulverizer thought.

That voice sounds familiar.

Dribble!

Princess Pulverizer ran over to the open window and peered between the metal bars.

Sure enough, the big green dragon was seated in the corner with a giant bandage over one of his feet.

What had happened to him?

Lucas was in the cottage as well. He was

standing right next to Dribble.

Okay, so now Princess Pulverizer knew where her friends were. What she didn't know was how they got there. Or why the magic arrow had brought her to this place to find them. Unless . . .

Princess Pulverizer suddenly remembered something her father had once told her. He'd said it didn't matter if people lived in a cottage or a castle. Home was where your family was.

King Alexander had also explained that there were all kinds of families. Which, the princess figured, had to include friends who looked out for one another. So as long as they were together on this Quest of Kindness, Dribble and Lucas were her family.

One day, when the Quest of Kindness

had finished, perhaps the arrow would bring all three of them back to Empiria. But today it had directed her to this tiny cottage in an apple orchard where her friends—her *family*—were.

"I never said I was afraid of bugs!" Sir Surly shouted angrily at Dribble. "I said I didn't like them. There's a difference. And anyway, shut that big snout of yours."

"No," Dribble argued. "You're not the boss of me."

"Yes I am. The minute you stepped in that mole trap, you became mine," Sir Surly told him. "I caught you. And I can tell you what to do!"

A mole trap. So that's how Dribble injured his foot.

"You are all mine. Everything here is

mine. Mine. Mine. Mine." Sir Surly began jumping up and down.

"We get the point." Dr. Cuspid sighed heavily.

The folks in the cottage held their noses. So did Princess Pulverizer. The dentist's onion breath was *really* awful.

"Even the apple orchard is mine," Sir Surly told Dribble and Lucas. "At least it is now. These trees used to belong to the King of Yabko-kokomo."

"*Used* to?" Lucas asked him nervously.

Sir Surly nodded proudly. "I wanted this orchard. So I took it. And it was the easiest thing I've ever done. I just slapped up a few signs and started a rumor about the woods being too dangerous to enter."

"What kind of rumor?" Dribble asked suspiciously.

Sir Surly laughed. "You don't actually think there's a Yabko-kokomo Beast, do you?"

"Isn't there?" Lucas wondered aloud.

"Nah." Sir Surly laughed. "I started that rumor. And those fools believed it."

"Why would you do that?" Dribble asked him.

"So they would be afraid to come into the orchard and search for my prisoners," Sir Surly said. "Even the Yabko-kokomo knights are too scared to come here."

Princess Pulverizer was shocked. Nothing—not even a *real* beast—would stop her father's knights from doing *their* duty.

"But the orchard should belong to the whole kingdom," Lucas insisted. "So everyone can share the apples."

"Do I look like the kind of guy who

shares?" Sir Surly demanded. "I worked hard for that king. And what did I get in return? A new shield? A sword? That's nothing. I earned this orchard. And if the king wasn't going to give it to me, I had to take it."

Lucas shook his head. "Knights don't do good deeds so they can get things. Knights are selfless. And noble. Or at least they should be."

"Oh please." Sir Surly groaned. "You don't know what it's like to be a knight. You don't know *anything*. You didn't even know enough to run away when I captured that dragon."

"I would never leave Dribble when he's in trouble," Lucas said. "He's my friend."

Princess Pulverizer was impressed. Staying with Dribble took guts. Lucas wasn't so lily-livered after all.

"Yeah, well, now *you're* mine, too," Sir Surly told Lucas. "And you're gonna help me build traps to catch the beady-eyed moles that are stealing *my* apples. And when we catch them, we're gonna have mole stew for dinner!"

"That sounds disgusting," Lucas said.

"It will be," Nate Jape agreed. "*Everything* Madame Zucker makes is disgusting."

"I don't know how someone like *you* ever got to be a knight," Dribble told Sir Surly.

"It was easy," Sir Surly boasted. "I saved a princess from an avalanche in the village of BialyBogen. That was a deed worthy of being knighted."

Princess Pulverizer's sword began to quiver at her side. The sword had magical powers. It always trembled when someone lied. Sir Surly was clearly not telling the truth.

"That's impossible," Dribble told him. "I've been to BialyBogen. It's a dry, flat, sandy desert. You need snow and hills to have an avalanche."

Sir Surly laughed haughtily. "I'm glad the King of Yabko-kokomo didn't know that. He believed my whole story."

"You've probably never even been to BialyBogen," Dribble grumbled.

"I haven't," Sir Surly

agreed. "But that doesn't matter. What matters is the king *believed* I had been there. I'm very good at getting people to believe what I tell them."

Sssssss . . .

Suddenly, a hissing sound came from behind where Sir Surly was standing. Princess Pulverizer craned her neck to better see what was happening.

"AAAAHHHHH!" Sir Surly jumped up onto a nearby chair. "Snake! Snake!"

Nate Jape started laughing.

Sir Surly stopped screaming and looked around. There was no snake.

Only a small, roundish boy with a big grin on his face.

"Not funny, Nate," Sir Surly said. "I don't like

practical jokes. Have you forgotten why I kidnapped you in the first place?"

"Because you don't have a good sense of humor?" Nate suggested.

"No, as punishment for pulling my chair out from under me at the tavern," Sir Surly reminded him. "The other knights laughed at me. I don't like being laughed at."

"It was funny," Nate insisted.

"You won't think it's funny years from now when you're still my prisoner," Sir Surly told

him. "No one will ever come looking for any of you. They're all too afraid."

Lucas let out a sob. Dribble gently rested a big claw on his pal's shoulder.

The princess gritted her teeth. Sir Surly was wrong. Someone *was* going to rescue his prisoners. And that someone was Princess Pulverizer! She was determined to free them all.

The question was *how*.

CHAPTER 5

Think. Think. Think.

Princess Pulverizer had been certain
that she would awaken with a great idea
for rescuing all of Sir Surly's prisoners.
But the sun was now shining through the
leaves of the tree where she'd fallen asleep,
and she had no plan at all.

Sir Surly would be a worthy opponent.
He wasn't just mean. He was smart, too.
He'd fooled a king and his knights into

fearing an imaginary beast! One wrong move, and she could become the next prisoner in that cottage.

"YOU! DRAGON!"

Princess Pulverizer was startled by Sir Surly's shouts from inside the cottage.

"Kill that spider! Now!" the evil knight demanded.

"You're such a baby," the princess heard Dribble snort.

"You won't think I'm a baby when I

slay you," Sir Surly snarled at Dribble. "Which is exactly what I'm going to do if you don't kill that spider. Don't think I won't."

Princess Pulverizer's magic sword didn't move at all. Sir Surly was telling the truth. He would slay Dribble if given the chance.

Things were really getting bad in there. There was no time to waste. Princess Pulverizer had to come up with a plan to rescue Dribble and Lucas, fast.

She wished she could just go back to Yabko-kokomo and tell the knights that there was no beast, and it was safe to go into the orchard and rescue Sir Surly's prisoners. But why would they believe her? They didn't even know her.

"AAAAHHHHHH! There's a snake in the cupboard!" Sir Surly exclaimed from inside his cottage. "Somebody get rid of that thing!"

Princess Pulverizer laughed in spite of herself. It was too bad she couldn't bring a whole army of spiders and snakes into the orchard. *That* would make the evil knight fall to his knees. But there was no way one person could drag that many spiders and snakes into one place.

Or was there?

Knock. Knock.

It wasn't until the following day that Princess Pulverizer arrived once again at the front door of Sir Surly's cottage. She was sorry to have left Dribble and Lucas with the evil knight for so long, but some plans took time. And craftiness.

Knock. Knock. Princess Pulverizer pounded harder on the door. "Hello?" she called out. "Anybody home?"

The princess heard rustling inside the cottage. Then she heard armor clanking and footsteps stomping.

Finally, the door swung open.

"WHO DARES TO DISTURB SIR SURLY?"

Princess Pulverizer looked up at the evil knight. His face was tight and angry. He seemed poised for a fight. *This* was one scary guy.

But the princess refused to let Sir Surly know she was frightened. That would give him a great advantage.

Instead, she forced herself to smile. "It's really you!" she squealed. "Sir Surly!"

"Who else would I be?" the knight demanded.

"I'm so excited to meet you. I'm your biggest fan. In fact, I'm president of the Sir Surly Fan Club."

Princess Pulverizer's sword began to shake. It knew what a big lie that was.

"I have a fan club?" Sir Surly asked, amazed. "I mean, *of course* I have a fan club. I'm fantastic!"

"Ever since I heard the story of how you rescued the princess of BialyBogen, I have been just dying to meet you," Princess Pulverizer told him.

"I never saved . . . ," Sir Surly began. Then he caught himself. "I mean, I never thought of myself while I was in that avalanche. I thought only of the princess's safety. I am a very brave knight."

Talk about a lie! Princess Pulverizer's truth-telling sword was practically dancing now.

The princess forced herself to smile even more brightly. "And that's why I brought you a gift," she told him.

Sir Surly looked surprised. And *thrilled*. "It's about time someone found me deserving of gifts for my bravery."

"Oh, I think you should get *everything* you deserve," Princess Pulverizer agreed. And this time her sword did not quiver a bit. "That's why I made you this."

The princess stepped aside to reveal a clay piñata she'd sculpted in the shape of Sir Surly's head. It was hanging from the branch of a nearby tree.

"What is *that*?" Sir Surly asked.

"It's a piñata," Princess Pulverizer replied simply.

"Is that supposed to be my face?" Sir Surly demanded.

"Yes," Princess Pulverizer said.

"That doesn't look a thing like me," Sir Surly continued. "It's hideous."

Sir Surly wasn't wrong. It *was* pretty awful-looking. But that wasn't the point.

"The piñata is filled with treasures," Princess Pulverizer assured him.

"What kinds of treasures?" Sir Surly demanded.

"Don't you want to be surprised?" Princess Pulverizer offered Sir Surly a big stick and a blindfold. "Why don't you break it open?"

Sir Surly yanked the stick and the cloth from her hand and threw them to the ground. "Why would I want to play some children's game?" he scoffed. The evil knight stepped out of his cottage, locked the door, and stormed over to the tree. He rubbed his hands together excitedly. "Let's see what kinds of treasures will be mine . . . all mine!"

Sir Surly yanked powerfully at the piñata's pointy nose.

CRACK! The clay piñata broke into pieces.

The treasures fell to the ground.

And Sir Surly let out a scream that echoed throughout the entire orchard. "AAAAAAHHHHH!"

CHAPTER 6

Spiders fell from every crack in the broken piñata. They crept and crawled onto Sir Surly's arms and legs.

Snakes slithered out of the clay and down onto the ground. They hissed angrily as they circled Sir Surly's feet.

"AAAHHH!" Sir Surly shouted again. "Get these things away from me."

Princess Pulverizer waited for the knight to swat the spiders and step

away from the snakes. But he didn't. He *couldn't*. He was frozen with fear.

That was exactly the response Princess Pulverizer had been hoping for. Quickly, she raced over to the cottage and tried to free Sir Surly's prisoners.

But she'd forgotten about the lock on the door.

Princess Pulverizer could see that Sir Surly was wearing a key on his belt. But she didn't dare grab for it. That might bring him back from his fearful state.

So Princess Pulverizer stared at the lock.

She poked her finger in the keyhole.

She kicked at the door. But it would not open.

A small hand poked through the window bars. "Are you looking for this?"

Nate Jape asked, dangling a key. "It's his extra one."

Princess Pulverizer reached for the key.

But Nate yanked it back inside. "You're too slow." He laughed. "Try again."

Princess Pulverizer was not in a kidding mood. "Do you want to be stuck in there forever?" she demanded.

"Sheesh," Nate said as he dropped the key out the window. "Can't anyone around here take a joke?"

Princess Pulverizer picked up the key and opened the lock. "Run!" she shouted as she flung the door open. "Now's your chance!"

Madame Zucker, Dr. Cuspid, and Nate Jape did not waste a single second. They all ran for the door at the same time, pushing and shoving in the hopes of being first out of the cottage. Finally, the three of them spilled out, leaped to their feet, and scurried away as fast as they could, without even a nod of thanks.

But Dribble and Lucas didn't leave. They stood right by Princess Pulverizer's side.

"I'm glad to see you," Lucas said. "I thought we were going to spend the rest of our lives in that cottage!"

"He kept threatening to slay me," Dribble added. "It was awful."

"We're lucky Sir Surly is such a big chicken," Princess Pulverizer said. "Look at him. He's scared stiff."

"Wanna bet?" Sir Surly shouted out furiously.

Apparently being called a chicken was all it took to shock Sir Surly out of his frozen state. The angry knight drew his sword and lunged at Princess Pulverizer.

But Princess Pulverizer was quick. She drew *her* sword, ready to duel.

Well, sort of ready. The truth was, Princess Pulverizer had never done any actual sword fighting before.

But the princess had certainly seen plenty of fights. She used to watch the boys in Knight School practicing with their swords. It didn't seem that hard. It looked kind of like dancing. Well, dancing

with a sharp, pointed weapon in your
hand.

Which was a bit of a problem.

Sir Surly was protected by a full suit of
armor. But Princess Pulverizer wore only a
plain cloth tunic. She had nothing but her
sword to defend herself.

Sir Surly lunged at Princess Pulverizer.

Princess Pulverizer danced backward—tap, tap, hop.

She lunged at Sir Surly—hop, hop, jab!

Sir Surly twisted his body away. "I'm an expert swordsman," he boasted. "This is your *unlucky* day. Say goodbye and prepare to die!" He thrust his sword right toward the princess's chest.

Princess Pulverizer pivoted out of reach of the oncoming sword.

Which left Lucas right in its path.

"Yikes!" Lucas leaped backward, trying to get out of the way. "WHOA!" he exclaimed as he fell down into a giant mole hole.

"Lucas!" Dribble called to him. "Are you okay?"

"I'm fine," Lucas replied. "That last step was a doozy!"

Princess Pulverizer wanted to help Lucas out of the hole. But she didn't dare turn away from Sir Surly.

"Take that," Princess Pulverizer called out as she rammed her sword at Sir Surly's arm.

He raised his sword to stop her.

The clicking and clacking of their blades echoed through the hills.

Click. Clack. Click. Clack.

Princess Pulverizer danced forward. Tap, tap, lunge.

Sir Surly moved backward, edging closer and closer to a nearby tree trunk.

"You really have your back against the wall now," Princess Pulverizer taunted.

She poked at his shoulder with her sword.

"Oh please." Sir Surly laughed haughtily. "Do you think I can be defeated by a *kid*?"

That did it! If Princess Pulverizer had been angry before, she was furious now. She moved her foot to advance toward him. But before she could take that step—

"What the—" Sir Surly began. But he couldn't finish his sentence. He couldn't even breathe. The air was being squeezed right out of him by a snake that had slithered up his leg and was now circling his belly.

The knight dropped his sword and tried in vain to loosen the snake's grip.

Quickly, Dribble raced over and grabbed the sword for safekeeping. "Now's your chance!" the dragon told Princess Pulverizer. "Get him!"

The princess looked at her sword. Then she looked at Sir Surly. His face was turning blue as the snake gripped him tighter and tighter.

She couldn't do it. She couldn't hurt someone who didn't have the ability to defend himself. Not even someone as evil as Sir Surly.

So instead, Princess Pulverizer grabbed the thick rope she had used to hang her piñata and swiftly tied Sir Surly to the tree. The knight twisted back and forth as the princess's speedy fingers created strong, unbreakable knots.

Once the princess was certain Sir Surly wasn't going anywhere, she gently unwrapped the snake from around his belly. She was very careful to keep her distance, just in case the creature got any ideas about wrapping itself around *her* instead.

She walked over and placed the snake on a rock in the orchard. "Go catch yourself a delicious dinner," Princess Pulverizer told the snake. "A Sir Surly supper would probably have just given you a bad case of indigestion. He's very *distasteful*!"

"Wow!" Dribble exclaimed when Princess Pulverizer returned. "Where did you learn to fence like that?"

Princess Pulverizer grinned. "The Royal School of Ladylike Manners. Only my teacher called it dancing."

"You're going to be sorry you did this," Sir Surly shouted to the princess. "Just wait until I get out of here."

"You're not going anywhere," Princess Pulverizer told him. "Those knots are unbreakable. I learned to make them in macramé class. We used to macramé fancy handbags to take on our travels. But this is a much better use for those knots."

"Are you kidding? I'm—" Sir Surly began. Then he let out a scream. "AAAAAAHHHHH! There's a spider on my nose! That's it," he told the princess. "You are no longer president of my fan club."

"Come on, Dribble," Princess

Pulverizer said, ignoring Sir Surly completely. "Let's go tell the King of Yabko-kokomo that we've captured the 'beast' and that he's just a big old scaredy-cat dressed in knight's armor."

Dribble shook his head. "Aren't you forgetting something?"

Princess Pulverizer looked around. She had her sword, her arrow, her ruby ring, and her knapsack. She hadn't left any trash on the ground or . . .

The ground! Wow. How could she have

forgotten? *Lucas was still underground.*

"Lucas!" Princess Pulverizer called down into the hole. "I'm going to find something for you to grab onto. Then I can pull you out. Okay?"

There was no answer.

"I said, *okay*?" the princess called out again.

But her question was met with only silence.

CHAPTER 7

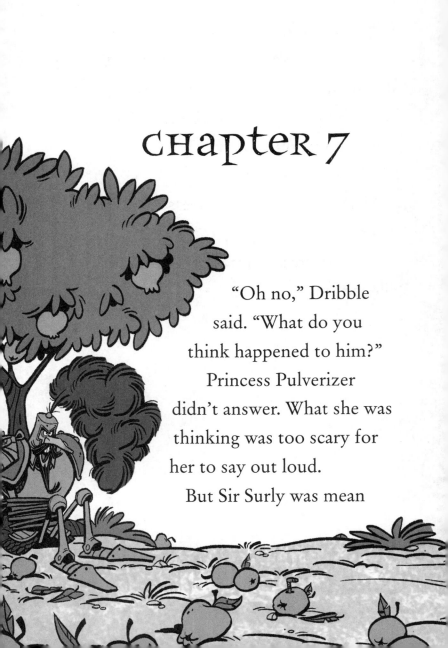

"Oh no," Dribble said. "What do you think happened to him?"

Princess Pulverizer didn't answer. What she was thinking was too scary for her to say out loud.

But Sir Surly was mean

enough to say anything. "Maybe there's
a monster underground," he suggested
as he angrily tried to twist his way out of
the rope. "Maybe your friend has been
captured. Maybe he's being held prisoner
in a dark cell with lots of creepy crawly
stuff all around."

Dribble's big
eyes grew even
larger. And if

Princess Pulverizer wasn't mistaken, they were a little wet and weepy.

"Don't start," Princess Pulverizer warned Sir Surly. "There's no monster. There's no beast. Lucas probably just went looking for a way out of the hole."

"And now he's lost and all alone," Sir Surly snarled. "And he probably has a horrible sense of direction."

"He does mix up his right and his left from time to time," Dribble admitted nervously.

"I have a *wonderful* sense of direction," Sir Surly boasted. "If you untie me, I'll go down there and find him for you."

"Not a chance," Princess Pulverizer said. "*I'm* going down there to find Lucas."

"Are you really sure you want to do

that?" Dribble asked her.

"It isn't a matter of *wanting* to do it," Princess Pulverizer told him. "It's what I *have* to do. I have to be brave and selfless." She turned to Sir Surly and added, "That's what real knights are like."

With that, the princess turned and headed straight for Sir Surly's cottage.

"Where are you going?" Dribble called to her. "The hole is over here."

"Your friend isn't brave at all," the princess heard Sir Surly sneer as she walked off. "She's leaving you here and your friend down there."

But Princess Pulverizer knew Dribble didn't believe him. Which was why the dragon showed no sign of surprise when she returned a moment later with a wax candle.

"I just needed to get something to help me see underground," she explained to the dragon. "Will you light it for me?"

Dribble opened his mouth and let out a tiny flame.

"Thanks," Princess Pulverizer said. "Keep an eye on this prisoner."

"Will do," Dribble assured her. He shot Sir Surly a menacing dragon glare—well, as menacing as Dribble could look, which wasn't very.

"Lucas and I will be back in no time," Princess Pulverizer said, trying to sound as confident as she could.

As she dropped down into the dark hole, she could feel her heart pounding furiously. She had no idea what was hiding beneath the ground.

The princess sure hoped she could find Lucas quickly. Before any more trouble could find *her.*

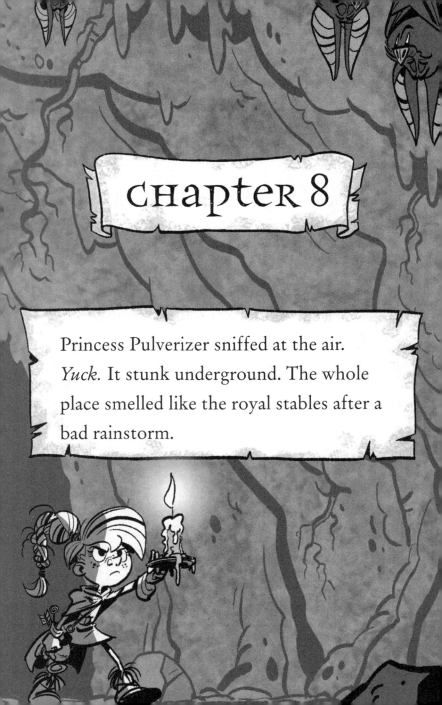

CHAPTER 8

Princess Pulverizer sniffed at the air. *Yuck.* It stunk underground. The whole place smelled like the royal stables after a bad rainstorm.

It was also chilly.

And very, very dark. Even by candlelight, it was difficult for Princess Pulverizer to see where she was going.

Not that she had any idea *where* to go. From where she was standing, Princess Pulverizer could see three different tunnels, each heading in a different direction. Which path had Lucas taken?

To the right?

To the left?

Princess Pulverizer frowned. If only there was someone there who could point her in the right direction.

Point!

That was it! The magic arrow had pointed her toward Lucas and Dribble before. Maybe it would do it again! She reached down and pulled it from her bag.

The arrow immediately pointed to the right.

That had to be where Lucas had wandered! Princess Pulverizer would find him any minute now. She began to stride confidently through the dark tunnel, holding her candle in one hand and the arrow in her other.

As she walked, Princess Pulverizer looked along the walls and listened for any cries for help. But there was no sign of Lucas anywhere. Where could he have gotten to?

Tap. Tap. Tap.

Gulp! Princess Pulverizer felt someone tap her on the shoulder.

Or make that some*thing*. Because that didn't feel like a human tap at all. She could feel sharp claws hitting her skin.

Double gulp!

Tap. Tap. Tap. There it was again!

Princess Pulverizer turned around ever
so slowly, and found herself face-to-face
with the biggest, fattest, hairiest mole she
had ever seen.

Yikes! That was one ugly rodent.

And if she wasn't mistaken, there were things crawling around on top of his head. She held her candle closer to get a better look.

Oh, gross! The mole was wearing a hat of knotted worms. It looked a little like a crown. Which could only mean one thing. This wasn't just any mole. This was the mole *king*.

The princess studied the mole king's face. His long snout was quivering slightly. He definitely wasn't smiling. Then again, he wasn't frowning, either. The princess couldn't tell how he felt about her invading his kingdom.

What she did feel, however, was a sharp push at her back. She turned her head to see two more moles standing right behind her. They were probably the king's guards.

The mole king began to walk down a long corridor. The guards pushed hard at the princess's back. Clearly they wanted her to follow the king.

"Where are you taking me?" the princess shouted. Her voice echoed through the tunnel.

The moles didn't answer. Probably because they didn't understand her. Princess Pulverizer did not speak a word of mole.

The guards pushed the princess farther and farther through the dark tunnel. Princess Pulverizer's heart was pounding so hard, she thought it might burst right out of her chest.

What if they were taking her to a mole prison?

What if Lucas was waiting there for her?

What if neither one of them ever got out of this place?

The mole guards pushed the princess around a sharp corner and into what seemed to be a large room.

Princess Pulverizer put the arrow away as she held her candle out in front of her and looked around. "Whoa!" she exclaimed nervously.

The room was filled with moles.

Big moles.

Fat moles.

Thin . . .

No, there were no thin moles in here. They were all pretty chubby. And no wonder. They were surrounded by the largest bug buffet Princess Pulverizer had ever seen. (It was also the *only* bug buffet the princess had ever seen.) The moles were slurping their weight in slugs and centipedes.

Squeort! The mole king let out a loud squealing snort.

The other moles stopped eating. They looked in Princess Pulverizer's direction.

Then they began to snort and squeak as loudly as they could. It almost sounded like cheering—like she was their hero or something.

Which maybe she was. After all, Princess Pulverizer had captured Sir Surly. He wasn't going to be able to trap any more moles in the orchard. They were safe. And she was the one who had saved them all.

Princess Pulverizer smiled at the moles and nodded her head. She was happy to have been of service.

The mole king twitched his snout in her direction. Then he lifted a crown of knotted worms from the ground and placed it squarely on Princess Pulverizer's head.

Ugh. The feeling of worms wiggling

around in her hair was really repulsive. But she didn't remove the crown. She didn't want to insult the mole king.

Squeork! Squawk!

Suddenly a group of moles in the corner began making the strangest noises.

Another group stood on their hind legs—and began to twist.

The moles twisted to the left. They twisted to the right. Then they dropped to the ground and wiggled all around.

It was as though they were doing some sort of dance. A *worm* dance! And all that squeorking and squawking had to be mole music.

Princess Pulverizer could only imagine what Lady Frump might say if she could see this kind of dancing!

The mole king twitched his snout at the princess. He beckoned her with his paw. Then he twisted to the left. He twisted to the right. He twisted to the ground and he wiggled all around.

The princess did not want to dance with the mole king. She didn't want to be his queen, either. And judging by the worm crown on top of her head, that was what he was offering her.

"Sorry, I can't stay," she told the mole king. She started for the exit.

But Princess Pulverizer didn't get very far. The exit was blocked completely by mole guards. They were piled on top of one another, leaving no way out of the room.

"Excuse me, I've got to get through," the princess told them politely.

But the mole guards didn't move.

So much for being polite. The princess used her free hand to try to shove the mole guards out of the way.

But the guards didn't budge. They stayed there, piled up, blocking her from leaving. Like a giant, unmovable mole mountain.

Which meant Princess Pulverizer was trapped—the only human in a sea of dancing moles.

CHAPTER 9

OOMF.

Princess Pulverizer grunted loudly as she tried once again with all her might to knock the guards out of the way.

She pushed so hard that the worm crown fell from her head. But still the mole mountain did not move.

OOMF. She grunted even more loudly, pushing harder. The guards wavered just a bit, then steadied themselves.

OOMF! Princess Pulverizer threw her full body weight into the guards. And then . . .

The wall of moles began to break apart! The creatures tumbled from one another's backs and began running in the opposite direction.

"Wow! I guess all those push-ups came in handy,"

Princess Pulverizer congratulated herself. She flexed her muscles proudly and hurried out of the room.

Except it hadn't been the push-ups. In fact, Princess Pulverizer hadn't been the one to move the moles.

Lucas had moved them! And he hadn't even had to flex a muscle. All he'd had to do was bring treats for the mole guards. He stood there outside the room, throwing slugs, centipedes, and ants down the long tunnel with all his might. And the mole guards were hurrying to scoop them up and scarf them down.

Princess Pulverizer stared at Lucas in surprise. It was a brilliant plan. And he'd thought of it all on his own.

"Am I happy to see you," Princess Pulverizer said. She looked at the crowd of mole guards chowing down on bugs. "Bringing them treats was a great idea."

"No mole can refuse a juicy slug cluster," Lucas said. "The bugs weren't hard to find, either. Even in the dark, I could feel them running around."

"Why did you run off?" Princess Pulverizer asked him. "It would have been so much easier if you'd just stayed near

the opening in the first place."

"I was worried about you dueling Sir Surly," Lucas said. "I thought you might need my help fighting him off. So I went looking for a place where I could climb out."

"I managed to beat him," Princess Pulverizer boasted. "He's *our* prisoner now. Dribble is guarding him."

"Wow! You won your first duel!" Lucas congratulated her. "All by yourself."

"Yup." Truthfully, the princess had had more than a little help from a snake, but she didn't feel the need to tell Lucas that. She doubted the snake would ever take any credit—seeing as how snakes can't talk.

"How did you know I was down here? And how did you find me?" Princess

Pulverizer asked Lucas. "You don't have a candle to light your way."

"I couldn't see. But I could hear you asking the mole guards where they were taking you," Lucas explained. "Then I heard all that *oomf*ing you were doing trying to get out of that room. I just followed the sound."

"Where did you learn to do that?" Princess Pulverizer inquired.

"When you spend as much time with your visor falling down over your eyes as I do, you figure out how to get along using your other senses."

Princess Pulverizer laughed. Lucas did seem to have his visor down over his eyes a lot of the time.

"We gotta get moving," Lucas told the princess. "It won't take the mole king long to figure out you've escaped. Come on, follow me."

Even though Princess Pulverizer hated taking orders from anyone, she knew Lucas was right. So she followed him. *This time*.

As she ran off beside Lucas, Princess Pulverizer looked up, searching for an opening in the top of the tunnel. But there was no sign of daylight anywhere.

And to make matters worse, Princess Pulverizer and Lucas soon reached a fork in the road. One path went to the right. The other to the left. Either one might lead them to freedom. Or straight back from where they'd come. There was no real way to tell.

"I think we need to go this way," Princess Pulverizer said, pulling Lucas to the right.

"No, I think it's to the left," Lucas countered.

"Let's let the arrow settle this," Princess Pulverizer said. She began to reach into her bag. "It will bring us to where Dribble is waiting. I'm sure it—"

Lucas put his hand over her mouth.

"What are you doing?" Princess Pulverizer demanded. Only it came out "Wa r u din?" because Lucas's hand was holding her lips still.

"Shhhh . . . ," Lucas said, trying to quiet her. "They'll hear you."

Suddenly, everything went black.

"Now look what you've done!" Princess Pulverizer scolded him. "Your *shushing* blew out the candle. We can't see a thing. Not even my arrow. What are we supposed to do?"

Lucas didn't answer. He just stood there with his nose high in the air.

Sniff. Sniff. Sniff.

"What are you doing?" Princess Pulverizer whispered.

"Sniffing," Lucas whispered back.

"I can hear *that*. What I want to know is *why* you're sniffing."

"I'm trying to smell our way out of here," Lucas told the princess. He began pulling her through the darkness. "We have to go left," he insisted.

"How can you tell?" Princess Pulverizer asked him.

"I smell grass," he told her. "It's coming from over there. And that means we have to be near an opening in the ground that's right below an orchard."

Princess Pulverizer didn't like being told she was wrong. But she decided to follow Lucas's nose anyway. What he said made sense. And besides, it wasn't like she had any better ideas.

"See, the smell of the grass is getting stronger," Lucas told her as they walked hand in hand down the path. "And I think I feel a bit of a breeze. That has to be coming from above the ground."

"I feel it, too," Princess Pulverizer whispered excitedly. "We're getting closer."

A few moments later, a sliver of light poked through the darkness.

"I think we found an opening!" Lucas told the princess.

"Now all we have to do is climb out of here," Princess Pulverizer said excitedly.

Lucas shook his head. "We can't," he said. "The walls are too slippery, and there's nothing to grab onto."

Just then Princess Pulverizer heard a whole lot of footsteps—or make that *paw*steps—heading their way.

"It's the mole guards!" Lucas said.

"They're coming for us. We've got to get out of here."

Princess Pulverizer agreed. The only problem was *how* to get out.

Suddenly the princess remembered something Lucas had told her when they'd first met. He'd explained that knights helped one another. Being a knight was all about teamwork.

One of their team was still above ground. All Princess Pulverizer had to do was ask for—

"HELP!" she shouted up through the mole hole. "DRIBBLE, HELP!"

"DRIBBLE!" Lucas added. "WE'RE DOWN HERE. CAN YOU HEAR US?"

Bump. Thump.

Suddenly, the ground began to shake.

"The mole guards are getting closer!"

Princess Pulverizer exclaimed.

BUMP THUMP.

The ground shook even harder.

"No, wait," Princess Pulverizer corrected herself. "Those steps are too strong to be mole guards. They're being made by something bigger—like a dragon!"

Princess Pulverizer was pretty proud of herself for having figured that out. In fact, she was surprised Lucas hadn't complimented her on her excellent use of her other senses.

Then again, they were a little busy at the moment.

"You okay, little buddy?" Dribble shouted from up above.

"We're both fine," Lucas assured him. "But we won't be if we don't get out of here right away."

"Okay," Dribble told him. "Stay there. I'll be right back."

Crr-rr-ack. Princess Pulverizer heard something breaking. A moment later, a long, thick branch from an apple tree slid down through the hole.

"Grab on, you guys," Dribble told them. "I'll pull you up."

"You go first," Princess Pulverizer told Lucas. "I'll wait here."

"No way," Lucas said. "I'm not leaving you here alone. Dribble is strong enough to pull us both up at the same time."

"Okay. You climb up first, and I'll grab on behind you," Princess Pulverizer said.

Lucas began to climb up the thick branch.

Suddenly Princess Pulverizer heard lots of squeaking and squawking coming from

just around the bend.
"Hurry," she urged
Lucas. "The guards
are almost here!"

Lucas climbed
higher up onto
the branch.

As soon as
Lucas had left
her enough
room, Princess
Pulverizer climbed on
beneath him, wrapping her hands
tightly around the tree branch.

"Pull, Dribble! Pull!" the
princess ordered.

"Hold on tight," Dribble called down
to his friends. "Here we go!"

"WHOA!" Princess Pulverizer let out

a shout as Dribble yanked at the branch with all his might. She almost felt like she was flying up and out of the mole hole.

The next thing the princess knew, she was in bright sunlight. Safe above ground. *Way* above ground.

The princess was *flying*!

Dribble had pulled with such force that Lucas and Princess Pulverizer lost their grip on the branch. And now they were up in the air.

Thud. Clank.

And then they were down. Boy, was that a hard landing.

"Hahahahaha!" Sir Surly began to laugh. "That had to hurt."

Princess Pulverizer scowled as she stood up and rubbed her sore behind. She opened her mouth and started to say something snide to the evil knight. But then she thought better of it. She had far more important things to say right now.

"Thank you for saving me from the mole guards," Princess Pulverizer told Lucas.

"Thank *you* for coming down to save *me*," Lucas replied.

Ahem. Dribble cleared his throat loudly.

"Thanks, buddy," Lucas told him. "You got us out of there just in the nick of time!"

"My pleasure," Dribble said. "Glad to help."

"Mole guards have nothing on us," Princess Pulverizer said cheerfully. "Not when we're working together."

"The power of three is *really* powerful," Lucas agreed.

Dribble looked over at Princess Pulverizer. "What's that crawling around in your hair?" he asked.

Princess Pulverizer reached up and pulled a worm out of her ponytail. "How did that get in there?" Dribble asked her.

"Don't ask," the princess replied. "Now what do you say we get going? I can't wait to tell the folks in Yabko-kokomo that there is no beast. And that the orchard is the king's land again."

"Hey! What about me?" Sir Surly called

out. "You're not going to just leave me here with all these spiders and snakes, are you?"

"Oh, I'm sure the king will send troops to come get you, once we tell him where you are," Princess Pulverizer assured him.

"But it's going to be dark by then," Sir Surly complained.

"Then I guess the king will just have to send the *knight* shift, won't he?" Princess Pulverizer replied with a laugh, as she and her friends walked off toward Yabko-kokomo.

CHAPTER 10

"This is awful," Princess Pulverizer whispered to Lucas as she spit a piece of apple pie into her napkin. "Sir Surly was right. Madame Zucker is an awful baker."

"It's better than a banquet of slugs and centipedes," Lucas reminded her.

"Not by much," Princess Pulverizer insisted.

Burp! Dribble let out a belch. A

dragon belch. Which came with a little flame, *and* a little stink. "Sorry," he apologized. "Must be something I ate."

Princess Pulverizer leaned back in her chair and looked up at the stage where the King of Yabko-kokomo was sitting in his throne, droning on. "That guy sure can talk, can't he?" she whispered impatiently to her friends.

"With Sir Surly in prison, the apple orchard belongs

to our kingdom once again. And Madame Zucker has returned to bake apple pies for us all," the king was saying.

"Are you sure that one was a *good* deed?" Dribble joked, pushing the tasteless pie farther away from him on his plate.

"At least Dr. Cuspid was able to finally brush his teeth," Princess Pulverizer pointed out. "*That's* a good thing—for everyone in this kingdom who has a nose."

Just then, Lucas stood up.

"Where are you going?" Dribble asked him.

"Nowhere," Lucas assured him. "I just need to stretch for a minute.

We've been sitting for hours. My rear end hurts."

"Sit down," Princess Pulverizer whispered to Lucas. "No one is allowed to stand up until the king does. That's a royal rule."

"Oh. Sorry," Lucas apologized. He started to sit down.

But before Lucas could reach his seat, someone pulled the chair out from under him. *Clink. Clank. Clunk.* He landed right on his bottom.

Everyone turned and stared. Even the king stopped speaking. The only sound in the room was Nate Jape's hysterical laughter.

"That wasn't funny," Lucas hissed at the practical joker.

"Won't you ever learn?" Dribble asked him.

Nate shrugged. "Probably not," he admitted.

Ahem. The King of Yabko-kokomo cleared his throat to bring the attention back to himself. He rose to speak. "Now, will our three brave heroes please come up onstage with me."

Princess Pulverizer walked proudly onto the stage along with Lucas and Dribble.

"As a token of our gratitude, I present you with this golden mace," the king said, handing Princess Pulverizer a heavy metal stick with a golden apple on the top.

Princess Pulverizer took the stick graciously. Her knees buckled slightly. The mace was heavy. She probably would have been better off keeping the crown of worms as evidence of a good deed. They were wiggly, but at least they didn't weigh a lot.

"That is not just any mace," the king continued. "It is one of our crown jewels. And as such, it has magical powers."

Princess Pulverizer brightened. That was something the worms didn't have. At least she'd never *heard* of a magic worm before.

"The mace of Yabko-kokomo can be

used to heal the wounds of anyone who fights on the side of what is good and right," the king explained. "But a word of caution: It is important to be sure that the person you are healing really is a good person," the king warned. "If you try to use the mace's power on someone who is deceitful or evil, its magic will disappear."

"Thank you so much," Princess Pulverizer replied. "We're just glad we could rescue the prisoners and return your orchard."

"Now let the banquet continue!" the king declared.

As Princess Pulverizer and her friends walked down the stairs from the stage, the king continued speaking.

"The rescuing of our fellow countrymen reminds me of a story I heard when I was just a young prince," he said. "Once upon a time, there was a princess who was trapped in a tower by an evil beast. She had long, long hair, because no barber was ever allowed in the tower . . ."

"Uh-oh," Dribble whispered to Princess Pulverizer. "We could be here for hours if he starts telling stories. Do something."

"Like what?" Princess Pulverizer whispered back.

"I don't know. You're the princess," Dribble told her. "Find some royal way to get us out of here."

Princess Pulverizer thought for a minute as the king droned on. Something royal? What did that mean? Royal like at her father's court in Empiria? Or royal like at the mole king's court?

That's it!

"And her toenails had grown very long because she had no clippers. And her teeth were yellow and brown because . . . ," the king continued.

"Follow my lead," Princess Pulverizer whispered to her friends, handing the heavy mace to Dribble. She dropped to her belly and started wiggling her way toward the door—as though she were doing the mole king's worm dance.

Dribble and Lucas looked at each other. Then they looked at the princess.

"She's lost her mind," Dribble told Lucas.

"Come on," Princess Pulverizer whispered. "Try to stay as flat as you can."

Lucas shrugged. "It's worth a try." He dropped to the ground and began wriggling toward the door.

"Okay," Dribble agreed. He dropped onto his tremendous tummy and wriggled behind his pals.

The members of the king's court were so busy looking up at the stage where the king was speaking that they didn't even notice the trio wriggling like worms along the floor as they made their way out of the room. A few moments later, Princess Pulverizer, Lucas, and Dribble

were outside the palace gates.

"That was some quick thinking," Dribble said, complimenting the princess.

"Thank you," Princess Pulverizer replied. "I couldn't have taken another minute of that story."

As the three friends headed down the road in search of a new adventure, Lucas turned to Princess Pulverizer. "How do

you think the king's story ends, anyway?"
he wondered.

"They all lived *apple*-y ever after,"
Princess Pulverizer joked. "How else?"

THE QUEST
CONTINUES . . .

AND NOW, HERE'S A SNEAK PEEK AT THE NEXT

PRINCESS PULVERIZER

WATCH THAT WITCH!

"Step, step, lunge!" Lucas said as he took two steps to the right and then brandished a butter knife in the air. "Step, step, lunge. Step, step . . . *whoops*!"

Bam!

Princess Pulverizer put her hand over her mouth with surprise as she watched her pal trip over a rock and land smack on his bottom.

"Sorry," Lucas apologized to the rock.

Princess Pulverizer's cheeks turned purple.

Her eyes began to tear up.

She thought she might explode.

But Princess Pulverizer refused to let out even a teeny tiny giggle. Because that wouldn't be nice. And Princess Pulverizer was trying hard to be nice these days.

"You're definitely getting better," Lucas's best friend, Dribble the dragon, assured him.

"You really think so?" Lucas wondered as he scrambled to his feet.

"You should try the riposte next," Dribble said. "You almost had that move down yesterday."

Princess Pulverizer knew what a riposte was—a counterattack against an opponent who had just lunged against you while you were fencing.

Only there wasn't anyone lunging at Lucas.

Lucas was fencing against empty air.

With a butter knife.

And he was still losing.

Lucas held out the knife and gave it a quick thrust.

The knife flew out of his hand and landed squarely in the middle of a pear that was hanging from the branch of a nearby tree.

to be continued . . .

Nancy Krulik

is the author of more than two hundred books for children and young adults, including three *New York Times* Best Sellers. She is the creator of several successful book series for children, including Katie Kazoo, Switcheroo; How I Survived Middle School; George Brown, Class Clown; and Magic Bone.

Ben Balistreri

has been working for more than twenty years in the animation industry. He's won an Emmy Award for his character designs and has been nominated for nine Annie Awards, winning once. His art can be seen in *Tangled: The Series*, *How to Train Your Dragon*, and many more.